The Tiger, the Brahman, and the Jackal

AN INDIAN FOLKTALE

Retold by M. J. York • Illustrated by Jill Dubin

The Child's World®
1980 Lookout Drive • Mankato, MN 56003-1705
800-599-READ • www.childsworld.com

Acknowledgments
The Child's World®: Mary Berendes, Publishing Director
The Design Lab: Kathleen Petelinsek, Design
Red Line Editorial: Editorial direction

ISBN 9781614732211
LCCN 2012932436

Printed in the United States of America
Mankato, MN
July 2012
PA02123

 nce upon a time in India, a fierce tiger was caught in a cage. He was hungry, and he very much wanted to get out. One day, a Brahman happened along past the cage. A Brahman is a priest or a holy person.

"Brahman!" called the tiger. "You are a holy man and must feel compassion for lesser creatures. Won't you please open this cage and let me out?"

"Oh, Tiger," replied the Brahman, "I fear you will eat me if I let you out."

"I give you my word," said the tiger. "I would be most grateful if you let me out."

The tiger began crying cold, salty tears. The Brahman pitied the tiger and agreed to let him out.

The second the door was open, the tiger stopped crying. He sprang upon the Brahman. Now the Brahman begged the tiger not to eat him. "You promised you wouldn't eat me!" he cried.

"I said I would be grateful," replied the tiger. "I promised nothing else."

The tiger opened his mouth wide. Slowly, his long, sharp teeth drew closer and closer to the Brahman's throat. But at the last second, he paused.

"I will give you a chance to save your life," the tiger said. "You must find me three things that agree my actions are unfair. Or else I will come and eat you for lunch!"

So the Brahman set off to find three things that would agree with him. First, he met a pipal tree. The Brahman told the story to the pipal tree. But to his surprise, the pipal tree said, "Why are you so upset? People sit beneath my branches all day long and never thank me. Then they come and cut off my branches to feed their cattle. You should stand tall like me and accept your fate!"

The Brahman was disappointed, but he continued his search. Next, he met a buffalo. The buffalo was plodding in a circle, turning a wheel that brought up water from a well. The Brahman told the story to the buffalo. But to his surprise, the buffalo said, "Why are you so upset? When I gave milk, the farmer gave me the finest seeds and grasses to eat. Now that I am dry, I turn this wheel all day and the farmer gives me only dry straw to eat. Keep moving like me and accept your fate!"

The Brahman was disappointed
again. He looked down beneath his feet
and told his story to the road. He was
sure at least the road would agree with
him. But to his surprise, the road said,
"Why are you upset? I guide people
where they are going and make their
journey easier. But people trample me
and drop fruit peels on me all day. Lay
down like me and accept your fate!"

The Brahman was very disappointed.
He turned and started slowly walking
back to meet the tiger. Before he had
gone far, a jackal ran up to him.

"Brahman, you look as sad as a child with no supper. What is the matter?"

The Brahman told his story. At the end, the jackal shook his head, looking puzzled.

"Many apologies, Brahman, but I am so confused. Perhaps if you show me the tiger I will understand."

The Brahman agreed, and the two walked back to meet the tiger. The tiger roared in greeting. "Brahman, I see you did not find three things to agree with you. I'm going to eat you now!"

"Wait," said the Brahman. "The jackal is slow of wits and he did not understand my story. Let me retell it for him so he can give his judgment."

The tiger was hungry, but he agreed. The Brahman retold the story. At the end, the jackal shook his head again.

"My poor brain! I cannot keep this straight. You are the Brahman," he said, pointing to the tiger.

The tiger was annoyed. He shook his head. "No, I am the tiger!" he answered.

"So that is the
Brahman?" asked the
jackal, pointing at
the cage.

"No!" the tiger roared. "That is the Brahman and that is the cage." He pointed to the Brahman and the cage in turn.

"I think I understand," said the jackal. "The Brahman was in the cage and you came along . . ."

"You fool!" roared the tiger. "I was in the cage and the Brahman came along."

"Is that right?" replied the jackal. "I think I understand. But how did you get into the cage?"

"In the usual way," sighed the tiger. He was sure the jackal was the slowest creature he had ever met.

"Maybe I would understand if you show me," said the jackal.

The tiger grumbled a bit, but he climbed back into the cage. "Do you understand at last?" he asked.

"Now I understand perfectly," laughed the clever jackal, slamming the door shut and locking the cage. "And now everything is as it was before."

India

FOLKTALES

The Tiger, the Brahman, and the Jackal takes place in India, a large country in South Asia. A Brahman is someone of a respected social group in India that includes priests and scholars. A jackal is a wolf-like animal similar to a coyote. And you probably know what a tiger is already! There may be other words you don't know in this story, but that's okay. Just have your parents or teacher help you find the meaning in a dictionary. Or sometimes you can discover the meaning of a word by looking at the surrounding words and pictures.

The Tiger, the Brahman, and the Jackal is a folktale, or a well-known story that teaches its readers a lesson. Folktales often contain magical elements (such as this story's talking animals) and they are always entertaining.

One moral, or lesson, of this folktale is to not be gullible, or easily tricked. Two characters are tricked in this story: first the Brahman, then the tiger. The tiger tricks the Brahman to let him out of his cage. He says he won't eat the Brahman once he's let out. But as soon as he's free, we find out the tiger lied. But the tiger gives the Brahman a chance to live, by finding three things that agree the tiger was unjust, or wrong in his actions. Luckily for the Brahman, he meets the jackal, who, by playing dumb, tricks the tiger back into his cage.

So what's the moral of this story? Don't believe everything you are told. Especially if it is told by someone who wants to eat you, or trap you!

A B O U T   T H E   I L L U S T R A T O R

When Jill Dubin was growing up, she and her sister spent hours making paper-doll collections. Jill continued her interest in whimsical art and received her BFA from Pratt Institute in Brooklyn, New York. Her illustrations have appeared in numerous children's books. Jill combines colors, patterns, and textures to create her cut paper collages.